The Adventures of Pinkie

Midnight Feast

Maddy Rose

RED FOX

Pinkie came down one morning just as the post popped through the door. There was a letter addressed to her!

Pinkie was so excited. She ran to tell her mum and dad.

A MIDNIGHT FEAST

Pinkie....

You, ...
are invited to a sleepover at
Hattie's house. Please bring
something for our midnight
feast. Thank you!

P.S. Please bring warm pj's
and socks, your own pillow
and a sleeping bag

"**LOOK!** I've been invited to a midnight feast at Hattie's! Please can I go? Can I make something **PINK** to bring for the feast?"

"You're going to the Grampies' today, remember?" said Mum.

"**BUT...**" said Pinkie.
"Maybe they can help," said Dad.

Gran was dusting
when Pinkie arrived.
"I've been invited to a
midnight feast, Gran!" said Pinkie.
"Will you help me get ready, please?"
"Ooh, that sounds exciting. But first we have
to do a few chores around the house," said Gran,
and she tickled Pinkie with a feather duster.

First, Pinkie helped Gran hoover to music.

Then Gran decided she needed some new curtains.

"Let's go to the haberdasher's to order some fabric," she said.
"**BUT...**" said Pinkie.

Pinkie liked looking at all the buttons in the shop.
Finally, Gran was ready to go home.
But first she said they needed some fruit.
"**BUT...**" said Pinkie.
"For your midnight feast treats," Gran explained.
"**YAY!**" said Pinkie.

Grandad had lots of fruit in his garden.
He gave Pinkie some apples for her
treats. "Thanks, Grandad,"
said Pinkie.

Pinkie and Gran worked hard all afternoon. They made pink cupcakes and "midnight feast specials".

Mum arrived at six o'clock to take Pinkie to Hattie's house. Pinkie couldn't wait to see everyone!

Hattie threw open the door and shouted,
"HELLO, EVERYONE! COME AND SEE!"

Everyone **RACED** out to the garden.

"**LOOK!**" said Hattie. "That's where we are going
to sleep tonight!"
In the middle of the garden were Hattie and Pinkie's
dads and the pinkest, floweriest Indian tepee.
"Hope you like it," said Pinkie's dad.
"So that's what Dad's been busy doing all day,"
giggled Pinkie.

IT WAS FABULOUS!

Hattie's mum made everyone
hot cocoa in the tepee.
Then everyone's mum and
dad said goodnight, and . . .

. . . Pinkie started telling **SCARY** stories
about Pirate Bess.

Then, Jazz and Ali told one about a two-headed bear.

And Hattie pulled the **BESTEST** faces when she told her story about a giant green sea monster who eats all the cakes.

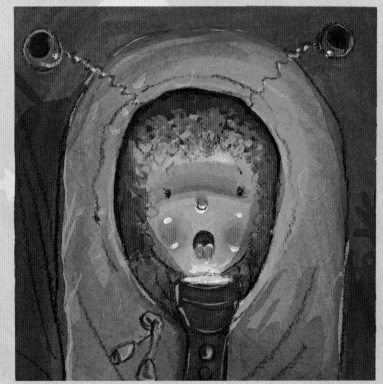

Finally, Pinkie said, "Let's have our midnight feast! What did everyone bring?" "It's **NOT** midnight yet," said Hattie. But when they saw the special midnight feast treats that Gran had helped Pinkie make, **NO ONE** could resist!

After a while, all the munching and giggling got
softer, and everyone fell fast asleep. It was
the best sleepover party **EVER**!

To Jayne, the super mum!